Lost little fish

written by
Grandma Mims

illustrated by
Natalia Kravchenko

Lost Little Fish

Title: Lost Little Fish/Grandma Mims

Identifiers: LCCN: 2023910033 | ISBN: 979-8-218-20865-3 (paperback)

Published and Printed in the USA

First Printing Edition 2023.

Publisher: Kroboth Publishing

For my grandchildren, may your faith and determination lead you to your destiny.

Love, Grandma Mims

"However far a stream flows, it doesn't forget its origin." African Proverb

In calm waters lived a little yellow fish. Despite her size, Yellow fish had a heart full of love for her mommy and daddy.

She loved swimming with her friends. They would swim and play games like hide n' seek and fin ball every day. They felt happy and safe.

All the little fish knew not to swim near the rocks because of the dangerous fish that swam behind them. The little fish knew that if they ventured too close to the rocks, they could get hurt.

One day, Yellow fish was playing ball with her friends. Suddenly, the ball got hit very hard and it floated behind the rocks. Yellow fish was a fast swimmer. She thought that she could swim fast enough to get the ball from behind the rocks without being seen by the big dangerous fish.

But as soon as she swam behind the
rocks, she bumped into a big Scary fish.
Little Yellow fish became so frightened.
She yelled for her friends to help her,
but they were too scared
to swim behind the rocks.

Scary fish opened his mouth—and in went little Yellow Fish.

As little Yellow fish tried to get out, she heard crying behind her. She turned around and saw a Pink fish who was just as scared as she was.

Yellow fish had never seen a Pink fish before—and the Pink fish had never seen a Yellow fish.

Suddenly, Scary fish coughed
unexpectedly and the two
fish fell out of his mouth.

Yellow and Pink fish realized they were free, and here Scary fish couldn't see them.

They tried to figure out where they were, but nothing looked familiar. They had traveled far away from their homes while trapped in the Scary fish's mouth. They didn't know how to get back home.

They met fish they never knew existed in this new place.

As time passed, Yellow and Pink fish grew up and became a family.
This place had become their new home.

Yellow and Pink fish had a baby fish and named her Offspring. They told Offspring about their encounter with Scary fish and the family that they still loved.

Once again, time passed, and Offspring grew up. She wanted to travel and explore new adventures and see where her parents were from.

They gave their blessings for her to leave, and Offspring had many adventures traveling with her friends.

One day they swam into new waters and discovered the place where her mother, Yellow fish, was from. Offspring met her grandparents, and all the fish who knew her mother. They all had similar patterns just like her mother and they lovingly welcomed Offspring into their homes.

Offspring was overjoyed and told everyone how
her mother and father survived Scary fish.
Offspring felt so welcomed and loved, but in her
heart she knew she was different from
everyone—not just in her appearance, but in her
nature.

Offspring was an explorer and knew she couldn't stay. She shared her feelings and thanked everyone for their love and kindness. She promised that she would return again to visit and bring her mother, Yellow fish too!

Although they wanted her to stay, they wished her a safe journey.

Offspring took one last look at her mother's birthplace and knew she was forever changed. She felt overjoyed that she didn't allow fear to keep her from following her heart.

Made in the USA
Middletown, DE
16 June 2023

32707839R10018